o p q r s t u v w x y z

10|87
First American Edition
Copyright © 1984 by John Burningham
All rights reserved
Published in 1985 by The Viking Press
40 West 23rd Street, New York, New York 10010
Published in Great Britain by Walker Books Ltd.
Printed in Italy
1 2 3 4 5 89 88 87 86 85
ISBN 0-670-22580-0
Library of Congress catalog card number: 83-25979
(CIP data available)

cluck baa

John Burningham

THE VIKING PRESS
NEW YORK

cluck

baa

buzz

croak

quack

yap

hoot

howl

grunt

squawk

roar

moo

neigh

chatter

purr

abcdefghijklm